THE FABULOUS LOST & FOUND

AND THE LITTLE RUSSIAN MOUSE

WRITTEN BY MARK PALLIS
ILLUSTRATED BY PETER BAYNTON

NEU WESTEND
— PRESS —

D1203224

For Emily and Lucy - MP

For Hannah and Skye - PB

THE FABULOUS LOST & FOUND AND THE LITTLE RUSSIAN MOUSE

First Printing, 2020
ISBN: 978-1-913595-08-1
NeuWestendPress.com

THE FABULOUS LOST & FOUND

AND THE LITTLE RUSSIAN MOUSE

WRITTEN BY MARK PALLIS
ILLUSTRATED BY PETER BAYNTON

NEU WESTEND
— PRESS —

In the middle of the big city is a tiny
yellow building. If anyone loses anything, this is
where it ends up.

It is called the Lost and Found.

Mr and Mrs Frog keep everything safe, hoping that someday every lost watch and bag and phone and toy and shoe and cheesegrater will find its owner again.

But the shop is very small. And there are so many lost things. It is all quite a squeeze, but still, it's fabulous.

One sunny day, a little mouse walked in.

"Welcome," said Mrs Frog. "What have you lost?"

YA poteryala svoyu shapku
"Я потеряла свою шапку," said the mouse.

Mr and Mrs Frog could not speak Russian. They had no idea what the little mouse was saying.

What shall we do? they wondered.

Maybe she's lost an umbrella. Everyone loses an umbrella at least twice, thought Mr Frog.

"Have you lost this?" asked Mr Frog.

Zontik? Net
"Зонтик? Нет," replied the mouse.

Then Mrs Frog remembered something
that had been handed in a few months ago...

"Is this yours?" Mrs Frog asked, holding up a chunk of cheese.

Syr? Net. On vonyayet!

"Сыр? Нет. Он воняет!" said the mouse.

"Time to put that cheese in the bin dear," said Mr Frog.

"Maybe the word 'шапка[shapka]' means coat," said Mr Frog.

"Now where did I put that nice yellow one?"

"Got it!" said Mr Frog.

Pal'to? Net. YA poteryala svoyu shapku
"Пальто? Нет. Я потеряла свою шапку,"
said the mouse.

She was starting to feel a bit frustrated.

"We need to keep trying," said Mrs Frog.

Ne sharf.
Не шарф.

Ne bryuki
Не брюки.

Ne sviter.
Не свитер.

Ne tufli
Не туфли.

Ne solntsezashchitnyye ochki.
Не солнцезащитные очки.

YA poteryala svoyu shapku
"Я потеряла свою шапку," said

the mouse.

Ne dva velosipeda
Не два велосипеда.

Ne komp'yuter
Не компьютер.

Ne tri knigi
Не три книги.

Ne chetyre banana
Не четыре банана.

Ne pyat' klyuchey
Не пять ключей.

It was no good. A fat wet tear rolled
down the mouse's cheek.

"How about a nice cup of tea?" asked Mrs Frog kindly.

YA lyublyu chay. Spasibo
"Я люблю чай. Спасибо," replied the mouse.

They sat together, sipping their tea and all feeling a bit sad.

Suddenly, the mouse realised she could try pointing.

shapka
"Шапка!" she said.

"I've got it!" exclaimed Mrs Frog, leaping up.

"A wig of course!" said Mrs Frog.

Ne parik
"Не парик," said the mouse.

Ne krasnyy
Не красный.

Ne svetlyy
Не светлый.

Ne korichnevyy
Не коричневый.

Ne raznotsvetnyy
Не разноцветный.

Ne zelenyy
Не зеленый.

"What about this?"
asked Mr Frog, pulling back
a curtain.

Da
"Да!" exclaimed the
mouse.

Slishkom vysokaya
Слишком высокая.

Slishkom malen'kaya
Слишком маленькая.

Slishkom uzkaya
Слишком узкая.

Slishkom bol'shaya
Слишком большая.

"One hat left," said
Mrs Frog, reaching all
the way to the back of the
cupboard.

"It couldn't be this
old thing, could it?"

Moya shapka. YA nashla svoyu shapku! Bol'shoye spasibo

"Моя шапка. Я нашла свою шапку! Большое спасибо,"

said the mouse.

"Ah, so 'шапка^{shapka}!' means hat. Wonderful!"

Mr and Mrs Frog smiled.

And just like that, the mouse found her hat.

Do svidaniya
"До свидания," she said, as she skipped away.

"До свидания," replied Mr and Mrs Frog.

"I wonder who will come tomorrow?" said Mr Frog.

Mrs Frog put her arm around him.

"I don't know," she replied, giving him a squeeze,

"but whoever it is, we'll do our best to help."

LEARNING TO LOVE LANGUAGES

An additional language opens a child's mind, broadens their horizons and enriches their emotional life. Research has shown that the time between a child's birth and their sixth or seventh birthday is a "golden period" when they are most receptive to new languages. This is because they have an in-built ability to distinguish the sounds they hear and make sense of them. The Story-powered Language Learning Method taps into these natural abilities.

HOW THE STORY-POWERED LANGUAGE LEARNING METHOD WORKS

We create an emotionally engaging and funny story for children and adults to enjoy together, just like any other picture book. Studies show that social interaction, like enjoying a book together, is critical in language learning.

Through the story, we introduce a relatable character who speaks only in the new language. This helps build empathy and a positive attitude towards people who speak different languages. These are both important aspects in laying the foundations for lasting language acquisition in a child's life.

As the story progresses, the child naturally works with the characters to discover the meanings of a wide range of fun new words. Strategic use of humour ensures that this subconscious learning is rewarded with laughter; the child feels good and the first seeds of a lifelong love of languages are sown.

For more information and free downloads visit www.neuwestendpress.com

я потеряла свою шапку	I've lost my hat
зонтик	umbrella
сыр	cheese
он воняет	it stinks
пальто	coat
шарф	scarf
брюки	trousers
солнцезащитные очки	sunglasses
свитер	sweater
туфли	shoes
один	one
два	two
три	three
четыре	four
пять	five
компьютер	computer
книга	book
ключ	key
банан	banana
велосипед	bicycle
я люблю чай	I love tea
спасибо	thank you
парик	wig

красный	red
светлый	blond
коричневый	brown
зеленый	green
разноцветный	multicoloured
шапка	hat
слишком высокая	too tall
слишком большая	too big
слишком маленькая	too small
слишком узкая	too tight
я нашла свою шапку	I've found my hat
огромное спасибо	thank you very much
до свидания	goodbye

> "I want people to be so busy laughing, they don't realise they're learning!"
> Mark Pallis

Crab and Whale is the bestselling story of how a little Crab helps a big Whale. It's carefully designed to help even the most energetic children find a moment of calm and focus. It also includes a special mindful breathing exercise and affirmation for children.
Also available in Italian as 'Granchio e Balena'.
Featured as one of Mindful.org's
'Seven Mindful Children's books'

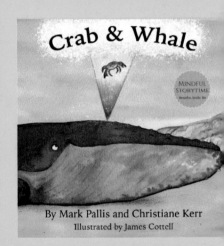

Do you call them hugs or cuddles?

In this funny, heartwarming story, you will laugh out loud as two loveable gibbons try to figure out if a hug is better than a cuddle and, in the process, learn how to get along.

A perfect story for anyone who loves a hug (or a cuddle!)

www.markpallis.com

Made in the USA
Monee, IL
22 July 2022

10156578R00024